The Turkeys' Side of It

J

The Turkeys' Side of It

Adam Joshua's Thanksgiving

BY JANICE LEE SMITH
drawings by
DICK GACKENBACH

HARPER & ROW, PUBLISHERS

The Turkeys' Side of It

Text copyright © 1990 by Janice Lee Smith
Illustrations copyright © 1990 by Dick Gackenbach

1 2 3 4 5 6 7 8 9 10
First Edition

Library of Congress Cataloging-in-Publication Data
Smith, Janice Lee, date
   The turkeys' side of it : Adam Joshua's Thanksgiving / by Janice
Lee Smith ; drawings by Dick Gackenbach.
       p.   cm.
   Summary: Disappointed at being cast as a turkey in the school
Thanksgiving play, Adam Joshua figures out a way to make the best
of it.
   ISBN 0-06-025857-8. — ISBN 0-06-025859-4 (lib. bdg.)
   [1. Schools—Fiction.   2. Thanksgiving Day—Fiction.]
I. Gackenbach, Dick, ill.   II. Title.
PZ7.S6499Tu   1990   89-78419
[Fic]—dc20   CIP
                                                                AC

To my mother, Olivia Lee—
because she never let the turkeys
get her down.

Chapter One

Everybody in Adam Joshua's class was looking forward to Thanksgiving, but they were all getting a little weary of the work.

"I don't think the Pilgrims had any idea what they were starting," Sidney said glumly, and they all sighed.

They made paper turkeys in art.

"If they'd thought about it, the Pilgrims could have just had more Halloween," said Sidney. "They could have all dressed up like ghosts and witches and handed out candy to the Indians."

They read stories about turkeys in reading.

"The Indians would have loved the candy," said Sidney. "The Pilgrims could have shown them how to carve jack-o'-lanterns too, and they could have sat around the fire and told ghost stories, and everybody would have been nice and happy without all the fuss."

Their math work sheets came with pictures of turkeys on them so that they could work dumb number tricks with poultry.

"Or if they didn't want more Halloween," Sidney said, "then maybe they just could have started Christmas earlier. The Indians would have been just crazy about hanging up their stockings and getting toys and computer games and everything."

All their spelling words were Thanksgiving words, and "turkey" topped the list.

"I just wish the Pilgrims would have thought about it more," moaned Sidney.

———

But then one day their teacher, Ms. D., looked them over and smiled.

"I know something you're going to be excited about," she said. "You're going to be in a play! If you'll hurry on down to the auditorium, the music teacher, Mrs. Cutwell, is waiting to talk to you about it now.

"Quietly!" she called after them, but everyone was so excited, quiet was the last thing on their minds.

Mrs. Cutwell was waiting for them, but she didn't look any too happy about it.

Adam Joshua didn't like Mrs. Cutwell, and he didn't think many other people did either, but they all tried to get along with her.

"It's a play about Thanksgiving," Mrs. Cutwell said, clapping her hands for the third time to get everybody quiet. "And there are parts for all of you."

Adam Joshua was glad that at least none of the other kids would have to be left out.

"We'll have the play onstage, and it will have a lot of singing and dancing while it tells the story of the Pilgrims and Indians together for the first Thanksgiving feast," she said.

4

Adam Joshua couldn't remember a thing about Pilgrims and Indians singing and dancing, but he thought Mrs. Cutwell knew best.

"You'll all have costumes," Mrs. Cutwell told them, "and we'll rehearse a lot. Then on the night before Thanksgiving vacation, we'll invite your parents and friends to come see the play.

"I'll tell you tomorrow what part you'll each have," Mrs. Cutwell shouted over all the clapping and cheering that was going on, "and we'll start rehearsing very hard."

Adam Joshua didn't think she looked nearly as excited about it as everybody else did.

———

Adam Joshua's dog, George, was waiting to hear about school the minute Adam Joshua got home.

"There's going to be a play!" Adam Joshua told him before they even made it to the front door.

George looked impressed.

"It's about Thanksgiving," Adam Joshua

told him, "and we get costumes, and everybody gets to come see it, and none of the other kids will get left out."

George looked relieved about all the other kids.

Adam Joshua went up to his bedroom with George and got out his book about Thanksgiving.

There was a picture of a Pilgrim named Captain Miles Standish. Adam Joshua knew he'd be great playing Miles. He thought Mrs. Cutwell was lucky to have him.

It took a fairly interesting struggle, but Adam Joshua finally managed to get George tucked up under his chin so he could see in the mirror how he'd look with a beard.

"Totally fantastic," he told George.

There was a picture in the book of the Indian chief Massasoit. Adam Joshua thought he was wonderful. He had paint stripes on his face and feathers in his hair. He was wearing a coat made of fur and leather moccasins, and he had beads around his neck and a tomahawk in one hand.

"Be right back," Adam Joshua said. He went into his parents' room and found some lipstick and a necklace. He didn't have any feathers, but there was a plastic flower, so he used that.

Adam Joshua drew lipstick stripes on his face, slipped on the necklace, and stuck the flower in his hair. He wore his slippers because they looked a little like moccasins, and after looking around for a while, he finally chose a toilet plunger for a tomahawk.

He stood in front of the mirror. Without a fur coat, he didn't look as good as he should, but he still looked great.

For the next several minutes, Adam Joshua worked hard at wrapping George around his shoulders to make him into a fur coat, and George worked hard trying not to be one.

They both fell in a heap on the floor, and George disappeared under the bed, outraged and disgusted.

While he was trying to catch his breath, Adam Joshua looked out his window and across his yard into Nelson's window. Nelson was over in his bedroom, looking ridiculous. He had on a plaid vest of his father's, his mother's pearls, and a leaf from a rubber plant.

"That kid doesn't stand a chance," Adam Joshua said, crawling under the bed to draw a lipstick stripe down George's nose too.

———

In class the next morning, a lot of people looked like they'd been wearing lipstick stripes on their faces the night before.

Adam Joshua's mother had made him scrub until most of his came off, but George still looked like he was on the warpath when Adam Joshua left for school.

———

Mrs. Cutwell didn't have to clap her hands even once to get everybody quiet. When they saw the clipboard in her hands, they got very still.

Adam Joshua hoped that Nelson would get to be one of the other Indians since he wanted it so much. He wondered if Chief Massasoit had an assistant and if maybe Mrs. Cutwell would let Nelson be one so that they could be together.

"Okay," said Mrs. Cutwell, checking her list. "Here we go."

Everybody held their breaths.

"Eric will be the narrator because he has a deep, loud voice," Mrs. Cutwell said.

Eric stood up. He bowed.

"Thank you," he boomed in a deep, loud voice.

"Next we need a lot of Indians," Mrs. Cutwell said, "and these people will all be Indians." She read off a lot of names, but she didn't read off Adam Joshua's and she didn't read off Nelson's.

"Ralph will be Squanto," she told them. "And Tyler will be the Indian chief Massasoit."

Ralph looked thrilled and Tyler looked terrified.

Adam Joshua let out his breath. He couldn't believe it. He started to raise his hand to see if Mrs. Cutwell had made a mistake, but she kept right on going.

"We need a lot of Pilgrims," Mrs. Cutwell said.

Adam Joshua held his breath again while she read the list.

"And Elliot will be Miles Standish, and Nate will be Governor Bradford," Mrs. Cutwell read, finishing the Pilgrims.

Elliot got his totally smug Elliot look.

"Adam Joshua, she forgot us," Nelson whispered, raising his hand.

"Now these people," Mrs. Cutwell said, shaking her head at Nelson so he'd put his hand down, "have a very important part."

Nelson put his hand down, and Adam Joshua sat up straight.

"These people," Mrs. Cutwell said, "will

play the parts of the harvest foods. And," she said, smiling, "they will do a wonderful Dance of the Harvest Feast at the end of the play."

Adam Joshua and Nelson looked at each other.

"Lizzie and Doug will be corn," Mrs. Cutwell read from her list. "Martha and Pete will be pies."

Lizzie and Doug started sliding down in their chairs. Martha and Pete followed them.

"Sidney will be a yam," Mrs. Cutwell went on, "Philip a pumpkin, Jonesy a lovely loaf of bread, and Susan a walnut."

Sidney, Philip, Jonesy, and Susan all slid down in their chairs.

"And finally, Adam Joshua and Nelson," Mrs. Cutwell said.

Adam Joshua and Nelson started sliding before she was finished.

"You will be the Thanksgiving turkeys!"

Adam Joshua would have said something to Nelson, but except for the other foods, everyone was laughing too hard for Nelson to hear, and besides—what could a person possibly say?

———

George was out, sitting on the sidewalk and waiting to hear all about it, when Adam Joshua got home.

He still had the stripe on his nose.

"I didn't get to be Chief Massasoit or Captain Miles Standish," Adam Joshua told him.

George looked a little worried.

"I didn't get to be any kind of Pilgrim or Indian," Adam Joshua said.

George started looking really upset.

"I get to be a stupid dancing turkey," Adam Joshua told George.

George looked truly horrified.

Adam Joshua sat down right on the cold, hard sidewalk and let George lick his face for a long, long while.

In an unfair world, there were days it was nice to get a little sympathy.

Chapter Two

The next morning, Mrs. Cutwell looked fierce.

"Okay," she said, handing around copies of the play, "down to business. Pilgrims and Indians need to learn their lines and speeches as soon as possible."

"Squanto has a lot to say," Ralph said, looking through the play and then looking proud.

"So does Captain Standish," Elliot said, looking around to make sure everyone knew it.

"Adam Joshua," Nelson whispered, "the turkeys don't get to say a word."

"I know, Nelson," Adam Joshua sighed. It seemed to him that the turkeys should have as much to say about Thanksgiving as anybody else.

"Excuse me, Mrs. Cutwell," Angie said, raising her hand. "I'm a Pilgrim woman and I hardly get to say anything. Hardly any of the women say anything."

"That's just the way it was," Mrs. Cutwell said. "The men did most of the business, so the women didn't say a lot."

"Well, my goodness," Angie said, frowning, "that hardly seems fair."

"Now then," Mrs. Cutwell said, placing chairs close together on the stage, "this will be the *Mayflower*, and the Pilgrims will act out coming across the ocean to America while Eric reads to the audience about it. Pilgrims, take your places, please."

The Pilgrims moved over to the chairs to take their places. Everybody fought for the first chair.

"Excuse me, Mrs. Cutwell," said Angie,

raising her hand. "I can read the maps if you'd like, on how to get to America. I just love to read maps."

"They would have read charts," Mrs. Cutwell said, "and the captain of the ship would have done it."

"Okay," said Angie, "then I'll be the captain, instead of a Pilgrim woman, and I'll read the charts and drive the boat."

"Angie," Mrs. Cutwell said sternly, "one of the men will read the charts. The women took care of the children, and took care of the food, and washed the clothes."

"That certainly doesn't sound like much fun," Angie muttered, frowning worse.

"Mrs. Cutwell," Jason said, raising his hand. "Some of the Pilgrims died on the *Mayflower*, didn't they? If you'd like I can die for you. I die really good." Jason put his hands around his throat, crossed his eyes, and let out a scream. He fell to the ground with a crash and died with his feet in the air.

"No dying," Mrs. Cutwell said, her voice

getting louder. "Eric will mention the dying when he reads, but we won't have any dying onstage."

Jason uncrossed his eyes and got back up.

"Yes, ma'am," he grumbled, taking his chair as a live Pilgrim again.

The Pilgrims practiced being on the *Mayflower* for a while. Some bounced and swayed. Some rocked and rolled.

"If you don't want me to die, maybe you'd like me to throw up," said Jason. "I'm also very good at that, and I'm sure some of the Pilgrims threw up."

"No dying," sighed Mrs. Cutwell. "No throwing up."

———

"At this point," Mrs. Cutwell told them, "as Eric reads about the Mayflower Compact, the Pilgrim men will gather around to sign it."

"'They agreed to build a new colony where they could be free,'" Eric read, deep and loud.

The Pilgrim men and Angie all came forward to sign the Mayflower Compact.

"Angie," said Mrs. Cutwell, "only the men signed the agreement. You'll have to go back to your chair."

"That's the silliest thing I ever heard of," Angie said, standing there with her hands on her hips. "Why didn't the women get to sign it?"

"It's just the way it was," said Mrs. Cutwell. "Sit down."

"Good grief!" Angie said, stomping back to her seat.

———

Adam Joshua and Nelson and all the rest of the foods sat and watched while the Pilgrims and Indians had a terrific time.

"I can't figure out what a yam does," said Sidney.

"Just about the same thing as a loaf of bread," muttered Jonesy.

Finally Mrs. Cutwell got around to remembering them.

"The Dance of the Harvest Feast," she said, standing there and looking them over. "Now, pay attention.

"I want the pies to turn in this direction," Mrs. Cutwell said, "with their arms out like this. Dip and glide," she sang out. "Dip and glide.

"And the corn and others need to whirl in this direction." Mrs. Cutwell showed them. "With their heads back and their arms up. Graceful and delightful," she sang. "Lovely foods to be thankful for."

"This woman's nuts!" Lizzie whispered.

"And now, the turkeys," Mrs. Cutwell said, smiling at Adam Joshua and Nelson, "are proud and dignified birds, and they must do a proud and dignified dance."

Mrs. Cutwell closed her eyes, put her arms in front of her, and swayed slowly. She moved around between the whirling corn and the twirling pies and looked a lot like a turkey.

"Adam Joshua," whispered Nelson, "she's

got to be kidding."

"Now you," Mrs. Cutwell said.

Adam Joshua and Nelson closed their eyes, held their arms out in front, and swayed slowly. They tried to dance between the whirling corn and the twirling pies. Adam Joshua ran into Sidney, and Nelson ran into Doug. Everybody fell into a food pile on the floor.

"Practice!" growled Mrs. Cutwell.

———

After school Adam Joshua practiced.

He put his little sister, Amanda Jane, and George on the bed to watch him, and he closed his eyes and put his arms out in front and held his head up high.

"Dip and glide," he sang. He swayed to the left and bumped into his desk.

"Graceful and delightful," he crooned. He dipped to the right and stumbled over a pile of junk.

"Lovely, lovely," he muttered. He glided forward and fell on the bed. Amanda Jane

crawled up on his back to sit on him, and George crawled onto his head to sit awhile too.

Out his window, Adam Joshua could see Nelson over in his room practicing. Nelson put his hands out in front and closed his eyes and looked dignified and proud. He dipped and swayed and glided and turned and only bumped into half a dozen things. When he was finished, he turned to his fish and took a bow.

"That turkey," Adam Joshua told Amanda Jane and George, pulling the shade down tight.

Chapter Three

Early the next morning, the foods got together for a meeting in the coatroom.

"I think we should go on strike," Sidney said. "If the corn and turkeys and yam go on strike, Mrs. Cutwell can't do anything about it."

"She can maybe take away all our recesses," said Nelson.

"She can maybe take away our Thanksgiving vacation," said Jonesy.

"She can clobber us," said Susan.

"Forget the strike," said Sidney.

Later in the day, Ms. D. called Adam Joshua and Philip up to her desk.

"You two are in charge of a poster for the bulletin board," she told them. "Make it a Things I Am Thankful For poster, and have everyone write in their special things."

Philip found markers while Adam Joshua went to get the biggest piece of poster board he could find.

"THINGS I AM THANKFUL FOR," Philip wrote at the top of the poster.

"George," Adam Joshua wrote, to start things off.

"My fish," wrote Nelson, and a lot of other people put the names of their pets.

"If I could get a dog, it would be a dog," wrote Ralph.

Everybody stood around trying to think of something else.

"THINGS I AM SOMETIMES THANKFUL FOR," Adam Joshua wrote on the poster.

"Amanda Jane," he wrote.

"Probably the new baby that's coming," Philip wrote.

Everybody wrote in the names of their brothers and sisters.

There was still a lot of room left on the poster. Everybody thought some more.

"THINGS I REALLY HATE!" Philip wrote at the bottom.

"Broccoli," wrote Adam Joshua.

"This play!" wrote Nelson, and all the rest of the Thanksgiving foods lined up to sign their names.

"Not exactly what I had in mind," Ms. D. said, chuckling when she came to see the poster.

"Mr. D. and teaching," she wrote under "THANKFUL FOR."

"My brother, Albert," she wrote under "SOMETIMES."

"The dark!" she wrote under "REALLY HATE!"

She underlined it twice.

———

That afternoon, they kept rehearsing.

Mrs. Cutwell kept yelling.

Jason kept trying to throw up or die.

All the foods kept trying to dip and glide and kept making a terrible stew of it.

Angie kept grumbling.

"Okay, this is your big scene, Pilgrim women," Mrs. Cutwell said.

Angie and Gabby and Heidi stood beside the big pot in the center of the stage.

"Stir, stir!" said Mrs. Cutwell.

———

Eric read about some of the foods the Pilgrims fixed, and the girls told about others.

"'Corn pudding and bread pudding. Fish and clams. Biscuits and berries,'" Eric read.

"It could have been worse," Jonesy the Bread muttered. "She could have made me a clam."

"'The Indians brought five deer to the feast,'" Eric read.

"And I suppose we're expected to cook those too," Angie grumbled, stirring along.

"'The women cooked and baked and fixed enough food so the feast could last for three days,'" read Eric.

"Somebody else had better be planning to wash the dishes," said Angie.

The foods got together for another meeting.

"We'll go to her and talk to her," said Sidney. "We'll tell her how embarrassed we are to be foods, and how disgusted we are, and how we just can't do it."

"She'd clobber us the minute we said a word," said Susan.

"Forget the talk," sighed Sidney.

Thanksgiving came creeping closer.

At home, there was a turkey from the grocery store in the refrigerator. It looked terrible without its feathers and worse without its head.

At school, they kept having rehearsals.

Adam Joshua talked to George every night.

"It's getting worse," he said.

"Mrs. Cutwell is yelling at us all the time, and making us dip and glide all the time, and every time we dip or glide, we fall down or crash into somebody.

"When we do it wrong, we look stupid," he told George. "When we do it right, we look worse."

George offered all the sympathy he could, but there was only so much a dog could do.

"Maybe today Mrs. Cutwell will change our part," Nelson told Adam Joshua each morning as they walked to school.

"Maybe tomorrow," Nelson would groan on their way home.

———

"Today we practice in costume," Mrs. Cutwell finally said. "Go find yours and we'll begin.

"I meant slowly," she hollered after them as they all stampeded for the costume room.

The Pilgrim men got to wear black suits and tall black hats with silver buckles.

"Although I should get the biggest buckle," Elliot said, swaggering around as Captain Standish. "I'll have to see what I can do about that."

"This is sort of what I thought we'd get stuck with," Angie said, holding up a Pilgrim lady's long black dress and bonnet.

"Maybe jeans weren't invented yet," Heidi said, shaking her head about it.

"All right!" the Indians all shouted, when they saw their leather vests and beads and feathers. They pounded each other on the back and war whooped it up around the room.

All the foods looked at their costumes and looked very embarrassed.

"I've never felt so stupid in my entire life," Philip growled, pulling on the costume that made him look like a pumpkin.

"Adam Joshua," Nelson whispered, "looking like a pumpkin would be fine. Looking like a pumpkin would be great. But Adam Joshua," Nelson whispered, holding up a costume, "I can't believe we're supposed to wear these."

"Hurry it up boys," Mrs. Cutwell called. "Everybody else is waiting."

Adam Joshua and Nelson put on their costumes with their backs turned to one another. Adam Joshua couldn't stand to see Nelson looking that dumb.

Everybody but the other foods howled when they walked onstage.

"Bluck, bluck, bluck!" said Elliot.

"Don't be silly," Nelson said, trying to look

dignified and push his beak out of his eyes at
the same time. "That's the sound a chicken
makes," he said, stumbling over one of his
turkey feet and landing flat on his tail.

———

"We finally got up our nerve to talk to Mrs.
Cutwell," Adam Joshua told George in bed
that night.

"Right after dress rehearsal while we still
felt awful. All the foods lined up, so she could

see how dumb we looked in our costumes, and we put our foot down.

"That isn't easy," Adam Joshua told George, "if you're wearing turkey feet.

"It didn't do one bit of good," he said.

Adam Joshua sighed, then lay awake a long time worrying before he fell asleep.

George sighed too, but being a little more practical, he skipped the worry and fell asleep right away.

Chapter Four

It was time.

Time for Thanksgiving vacation.

Time for the Thanksgiving play.

"I'll be in the audience tonight to applaud and cheer," Ms. D. said, as she shooed them out the door after school.

"She must be thinking of a different play," said Sidney.

All the foods stood around on the sidewalk for a last meeting.

"Bluck, bluck, bluck!" said Elliot, smirking past.

"Whatever," sighed Nelson.

"I've decided I'm going to be sick tonight," Sidney told everyone. "It's the only way I can figure to get out of being a dancing yam. At my house," he said, "being sick isn't much fun, but I'm desperate."

All the foods brightened up a lot at the idea of getting sick.

"That's great!" said Lizzie. "I had the measles once, and couldn't go out to do anything, so I'll get the measles again."

"I'll get something with a cough," said Jonesy. "I'm terrific at coughs."

"What are the Pilgrims and Indians going to do without the Thanksgiving foods?" Martha asked.

"Peanut butter," said Doug.

———

"I'm working on being sick right now," Nelson said as he and Adam Joshua walked home.

"I'm sorry, Adam Joshua," he said, as he turned off toward his house, "but unless you want to be sick with me, you'll just have to be a dancing turkey all alone."

Adam Joshua tried coughing the minute he walked in the door, and he looked pathetic and held his stomach for good measure.

"Cut that out," his mother said, flying past in a flurry with the vacuum.

She left him with cleaning cloths, furniture polish, and orders to dust.

"Don't worry, he'll be there," Adam Joshua said as he tied a dust cloth to George's tail and tried to get him to wag it across the furniture. "That sick stuff never works at Nelson's house either."

———

Nelson's mother drove them to the school early that night to get ready for the play.

"I tried, Adam Joshua," Nelson said, when he got in the car, "but my mother said we have so much company coming and so much cooking to do, she didn't have time for me to be sick."

"Break a leg," Nelson's mother said when they got out of the car.

"Do you think she means turkey or regular?" Nelson asked as they walked into the school. "Never mind," he muttered. "She probably wouldn't have time for either one."

———

None of the other foods got to stay home sick either.

"Who knew you could only get measles once?" Lizzie said with a sigh. She still had red marker measle spots up and down her arms.

They glumly watched Indians painting stripes on their faces, and Pilgrims pasting beards on their chins.

"I can't even sit down," Nelson said, padding around. "My tail gets in the way."

"I've never felt so ridiculous," Pete said, fluffing his top pie crust.

They peered around the edge of the curtain to look at the audience.

Adam Joshua could see his mother and father and Amanda Jane.

George had wanted to come, but he'd had to

39

stay home, and Adam Joshua thought it was just as well.

"My grandmother's out there, Adam Joshua," Nelson moaned. "No grandmother should have to see her grandson looking like a turkey."

———

The lights went down. The music went up.

Suddenly everybody backstage knew it was time to go onstage, and everybody started looking scared to pieces.

"I may really get sick, Adam Joshua," Nelson whispered.

The Pilgrims took their places, and Eric hurried out to stand at the corner of the stage.

The curtain went up. Eric opened his book and read in a deep, loud voice.

"'The Pilgrims were on the *Mayflower* for more than sixty days and sixty nights,'" Eric read. "'And a lot of them were sick.'"

"I can understand that," Eric said, looking up. "I took a boat ride once to see the Statue of Liberty and I threw up all the way."

Mrs. Cutwell was standing backstage beside Adam Joshua. She groaned and put her hand over her eyes.

All the Pilgrims sat on their chairs on the stage. Some bounced and rocked to show how bad the waves were. Some washed and cooked.

Jason put his hands around his throat and crossed his eyes and let out a scream. He fell to the ground with a crash and died with his feet in the air.

"I should have known," Mrs. Cutwell moaned.

"Anyway," Eric said, "'the Pilgrims thought they'd never get off that boat.'"

All the Pilgrims looked worried, and everybody patted everybody else on the back.

"'LAND HO!'" Eric shouted.

———

"'It was very hard trying to make a new home in Plymouth Colony,'" Eric told everyone.

The Pilgrims walked around looking cold

and hungry and sick and tired. Some of the audience, including Ms. D., looked sad.

"'Half the Pilgrims died that winter,'" Eric said.

Jason fell down dead again.

"Grr," said Mrs. Cutwell.

"'First, one Indian came to visit the Pilgrims, and then came others,'" Eric read.

"'WELCOME, ENGLISHMEN!'" boomed Squanto/Ralph. He walked onstage looking proud and important.

The Pilgrims and Indians stood together to sing a song about friendship.

"Lovely, lovely," Mrs. Cutwell whispered.

Ralph had a lot to do onstage, showing the Pilgrims how to plant corn with fish and how to hunt deer. He taught them how to find clams and what plants were good for what things.

He took his time about it.

"Good grief," Doug said backstage in his corn costume. "I'm going to be popped if it gets any hotter back here or he takes any longer."

"We're in no hurry," Sidney reminded him.

"Oh, yeah, right," said Doug.

Chapter Five

Finally, it was time for the first Thanksgiving.

"And the biggest lines we get in the whole play are all about food," Angie muttered, straightening her bonnet.

"I can't believe she thinks that's a problem," Jonesy the Bread said as Angie stomped onstage.

"'The women cooked and baked for days to get ready for the feast,'" Angie said, standing over the kettle and stirring to show she was working hard.

"'They fixed corn bread and pies and yams,'" Gabby said, stirring too.

"'And chowder and lobsters and scallops,'" said Heidi, stirring along.

"I love yams," Gabby said, interrupting and forgetting to stir. "At my house we always fix them with marshmallows and pineapple and put them in the oven for a long time."

Heidi glared at Gabby and kept talking. "'The men went hunting and brought back ducks and turkeys, geese and quail.'"

"So we had to cook all the stupid stuff the men brought home too," said Angie. "And none of it came in packages."

"Of course, the Pilgrims didn't have marshmallows," Gabby said, "but they might have done something nice with chestnuts."

The Pilgrim women stopped cooking and Heidi and Gabby made their exit from the stage. Angie reached in the pot before she left and pulled out a sign. She walked off the stage slowly and held the sign high so that everyone in the audience could see it.

"PILGRIMS UNFAIR TO WOMEN!" it read.

———

Mrs. Cutwell poked, pulled, pounded down, and fluffed up the foods' costumes, getting them ready for the Dance of the Harvest Feast.

"Smile like a yam!" she scolded Sidney, tweaking his cheek.

"I can't stand it if everybody laughs," Nelson whispered as they lined up. "I can take a lot of things, but I can't take that."

"What else do you expect them to do?" Sidney muttered through his potato grin.

An ear of corn and the pumpkin pie looked like fluffed-up foods doing their best not to cry.

Adam Joshua knew exactly how they felt.

"Listen," he whispered, "if they're going to laugh at us anyway, maybe we should try to make them laugh. If we make them laugh," he said, "maybe it won't seem so bad."

Jonesy waited until Mrs. Cutwell had plumped up his bread costume to make him

48

look fatter and gone on past.

"Sure," he whispered. "Anybody know any good food jokes?"

"Anyway, Mrs. Cutwell really would clobber us," Susan whispered, as she practiced puffing her cheeks out like a walnut.

———

All the Pilgrims sang a song of Thanksgiving.

All the Indians sang a song of Thanksgiving.

None of the foods got to sing a song, but Adam Joshua didn't mind. He didn't think the turkeys had much to be thankful about.

———

And then it was time.

"Dip and glide!" Mrs. Cutwell reminded them sternly. "Graceful and delightful! Lovely foods to be thankful for!"

She gave them each a little push toward the stage to help them on their way.

The rest of the foods danced out, dipping and gliding. Sidney stomped more than he swayed, and Lizzie turned a miserable red to match her marker measle spots and shuffled, keeping her eyes on the floor.

People in the audience looked like they were trying very hard to take it seriously and not laugh.

"Graceful! Delightful!" Mrs. Cutwell hissed at them from the wings.

Jonesy looked like he was doing his best to think of some food jokes.

———

It got very quiet when Adam Joshua and Nelson danced onstage.

Nelson dipped with his wing, and Adam Joshua tried to glide on turkey feet.

One man in the front row laughed out loud, and several people started to chuckle. Adam Joshua could see other people, even his own mother and Ms. D., smothering giggles.

"I knew it, Adam Joshua," Nelson moaned, stumbling into the Philip pumpkin. "I just knew it."

"I knew it," Sidney muttered sadly, "but I still can't believe it."

Lizzie started to cry very quietly while she shuffled, big tears sliding down into marker spots that turned into little red stripes rolling down her face.

"Proud! Dignified!" they heard Mrs. Cutwell hissing.

Adam Joshua tried to dip a wing, and he thought about proud and dignified, and he thought about not getting to be Captain Standish or any other Pilgrim, and not getting to be Chief Massasoit or any other Indian, and about wearing this stupid, stupid, stupid turkey outfit, and about Amanda Jane watching, and George waiting to hear, and about maybe losing recesses, and Thanksgiving vacation, and getting clobbered.

"Enough's enough," he said.

Then he tried giving a very funny little kick with one turkey foot.

People chuckled.

Nelson looked at Adam Joshua and gave a little hop. A few more people, including their fathers, laughed.

Adam Joshua took a deep breath and grabbed one of Nelson's wings.

"It's time for the Turkey Boogie," he said.

Adam Joshua and Nelson kicked high and bounced low. They flapped their wings and flipped their feet. They stomped and stamped and shimmied their best.

There weren't exactly names for the dances the other foods did, but Lizzie looked like she was doing something call the Bounce, Doug did the Wiggle-Bop-Whistle-Kick, and Sidney did the Fling-Jump-Flip-Twirl—Bounce a bit with Lizzie—Wiggle a bit with Doug—Advanced Moonwalk-Fizzle Twist.

("Which wasn't easy in a yam outfit," he said later.)

And all the rest of the foods danced a feast fit to remember.

People in the audience started laughing out loud, and then they started clapping along with the music.

The Indians charged in from offstage, war whooping it up.

The Pilgrims came in doing the Bunny Hop.

"Don't worry, Adam Joshua," Angie said as she bounced by. "We decided if we all danced, you wouldn't be the only ones to get in trouble."

Everyone ended up in a chorus line doing the Cancan, and they all shook their tail feathers at the audience—even the people who didn't have any.

The whole audience stood up and cheered and applauded, and Adam Joshua's father shouted "Bravo!" while Amanda Jane shrieked and waved.

"All right!" said Sidney.

"Fantastic!" said Jonesy.

"Thank goodness!" said Lizzie.

"They loved it, Adam Joshua," Nelson said, grinning happily. "Everybody just loved it."

"Not quite everybody," Mrs. Cutwell growled from behind them as she came out to take her bows.

———

The foods got in trouble, and it was big trouble, but it wasn't as bad as it could have been.

"Only because I'm too tired and too glad it's over to get too mad," Mrs. Cutwell sighed.

"And it was worth it," Angie said, after the rest of the class had gotten in trouble too.

———

"Happy Thanksgiving, everyone!" Ms. D. said, coming backstage as they were getting ready to leave. "Have a wonderful vacation."

"Don't eat too much you-know-what," she whispered to Adam Joshua.

"Only peanut butter," Adam Joshua told her.

He and Nelson put their turkey suits far back in the corner of the costume closet.

"I will never eat a potato again," Sidney said, stuffing the yam suit in the corner too.

"Or an ear of corn," said Doug.

"Or a walnut," groaned Susan.

"Well, I'm still going to eat pumpkin pie," Pete said, hanging up his costume, "but I'm going to try not to like it."

"My mother's taking all the foods out for pizza," Doug said. "She said they didn't have pizza at the first Thanksgiving, and they don't know what they missed."

All the foods hurried after Doug.

"I'll be there in just a minute," Adam Joshua called, staying behind. He shuffled through piles of Pilgrims' beards, old tubes of Indian war paint, and feathers from turkey costumes, until he found some paper.

And he wrote a note. It told about the dance they did at the end of the play and some of the reasons they danced it.

He pinned it to the beak of his costume before he left.

Thanksgiving came every year, and he had a feeling that the people who had to be turkeys next time might like to know.